AFRICAN SLAVERY
A Young Boy's Story

SURVIVORS

AFRICAN SLAVERY

A Young Boy's Story

Stewart Ross

WAYLAND

Text copyright © 2002 Stewart Ross
Volume copyright © 2002 Wayland

Book editor: Katie Orchard
Map illustrator: Peter Bull

This edition published in 2015 by Wayland

Dewey number: 823.9'14 [J]
ISBN: 978 0 7502 9635 9

10 9 8 7 6 5 4 3 2 1

Wayland
An imprint of
Hachette Children's Group
Part of Hodder & Stoughton
Carmelite House
50 Victoria Embankment
London EC4Y 0DZ

An Hachette UK company
www.hachette.co.uk
www.hachettechildrens.co.uk

Introduction

Modern Europeans first landed in the Americas at the end of the fifteenth century. They brought with them illnesses previously unknown to the natives of the Americas and the Caribbean. With no immunity against killer diseases, such as smallpox, a high proportion of the region's native population died. This created a severe labour shortage, particularly on the farms and plantations that the Europeans had established in Brazil and on the islands of the Caribbean.

European traders hit upon a new and singularly disgraceful solution to the problem. The idea came from the Portuguese, who had been importing slaves from North Africa since the fifteenth century. Early in the sixteenth century Portuguese and Spanish merchants started buying cheap slaves in West Africa and shipping them across the Atlantic to work in America. Later, the British, French, Dutch and others joined this inhuman trade in human cargo.

By the eighteenth century, the time when this story is set, the bulk of the slave trade was in the hands of the British merchants. British ships transported literally millions of African slaves to colonies up and down America's eastern seaboard, including 2.4 million to Britain's Caribbean possessions. At every stage – from capture in Africa to purchase in America – the trade attracted unscrupulous men of little conscience and even less humanity.

African Slavery: A Young Boy's Story was inspired by *The Interesting Narrative of the Life of Olaudah Equiano, Written by Himself* (1789), the first published account by an African slave taken to the New World.

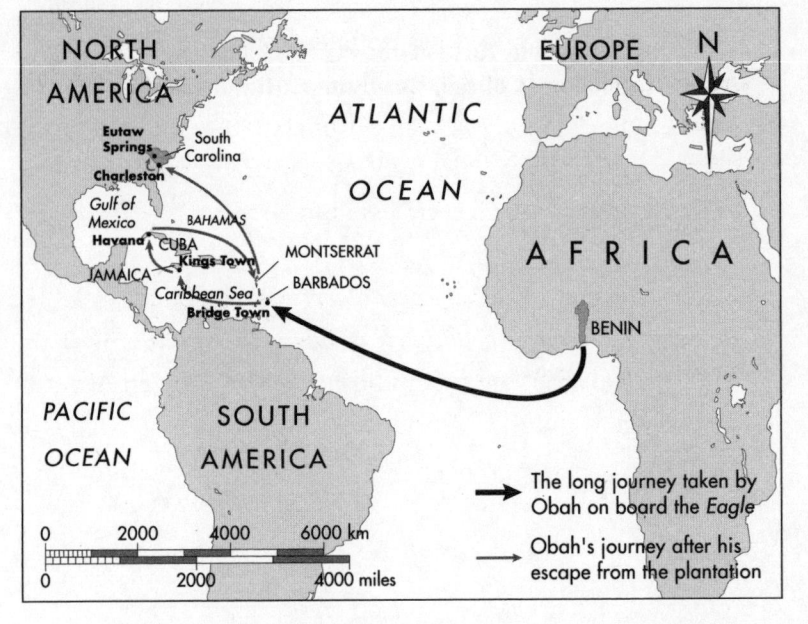

This map shows the long journey across the Atlantic
taken by Obah, the main character in this story,
and many other African slaves. We can also follow
Obah's route around the Caribbean on board
Captain Collins' ship, the *Dolphin*.

Dedicated to Turves Green Girls' School and
Technology College, Longbridge, Birmingham.

One

Beyond the Hills

I loved being up in the tree. Perched halfway between earth and sky, I wasn't a person any more, I was a bird or a cloud. The village shrank to a honeycomb of brown walls around little thatched huts. The people – my people – were the bees fretting from cell to cell. And beyond the hive were the dusty fields, the tangled forest, the purple-grey hills . . .

From the top of the tree I could not see beyond the hills. Nor had any of us ever travelled that far. I imagined, as we all did, still more villages, fields, forests and hills, rolling on and on for ever.

Not even in my dreams did I see what was really there: the shining sea and the bearded men in dark ships that sailed upon it. As a child my nightmares were of spirits and black beasts. Now I am haunted by white beasts, iron chains and wooden prisons poisoned by death.

1

You see, I have been taken beyond the hills. I know what lies there . . .

The tree was a lookout-post. At first light all able-bodied adults – men, women and slaves – set out on the long walk to the fields further down the valley. They sang as they went, their voices rising up into the sweet morning air. When we couldn't hear them any more, one of the older boys shinned up the tall tree that grew in our compound to watch for intruders.

Intruders? We didn't fear common thieves because we had no money or other valuables worth stealing. We didn't fear wild animals, either. But we *did* fear the 'Red People', the thick-set warriors with mahogany-coloured skins who came from the direction of the midday sun to steal the only thing of real value we possessed: ourselves.

Let me explain. Like all the Benin, we had slaves. Most of them, both male and female, were warriors captured during any one of the furious battles we fought with our neighbours. Although we didn't eat with our prisoner-slaves, we treated them well. They slept in our homes and did the same work as us. Some even had slaves of their own. Compared with the slaves who lived beyond the hills, ours were in heaven.

The Red People did not want captives to work in

their fields because they had no fields. They were kidnappers who needed strong and skilful bodies to sell for profit. Such a trade was alien to us and we hated all who pursued it. In our village, the penalty for kidnap was death.

When I lived in the village we captured only one kidnapper. It was partly my doing, too. I was taking my turn in the lookout-tree when I saw a stranger run out of the forest and climb the wall of a neighbouring compound. I raised the alarm, screaming at the top of my voice, 'Red Man! Red Man! There's a Red Man in Emoudiah's compound!'

Immediately, the older children ran to seize him. The Red Man sped back towards the wall, hoping to scale it and flee to the safety of the trees. But the children were too quick for him. They grabbed him by the heels, pulled him to the ground and bound him tightly with cords. Some of them wanted to cut off his head at once. But I said no, we should wait for the adults to return: only a meeting of the village elders could condemn a man to death. Although only twelve, I was the son of a high chief and a person of authority.

So we tied our prisoner to a post and left him to bake in the afternoon sun. We didn't give him a drink. Water was

3

too precious to be wasted on one who would be dead by nightfall.

The adults were full of praise when they returned. The elders gathered in our compound and called us to them. Sitting on the bench of scented wood reserved for high chiefs and honoured guests, my father declared, 'We are proud of you, children of the village. Your fathers are proud of you and your mothers are proud of you. In your hands our future is safe.' Then he turned to me and smiled. 'And you, Obah, my youngest son, is it true that you sounded the alarm?'

'Yes, Father,' I replied, staring at the honourable scars of leadership on his noble face.

'Then of you I am doubly proud,' he went on. He looked round at his fellow chiefs. 'It is a sign. As a child Obah watched over the village with the eyes of hawk; as a high chief he will he watch over it with the eyes of a leopard. That is my prophesy.'

How soon did his brave prophesy turn to bitter ashes in his mouth!

After the execution of the Red Man, we celebrated. First, the feast: two goats and half a dozen chickens cooked with pepper and other delicious spices, and yams, beans and plantain piled as high as my shoulder. When the meal was over, it was time to dance.

The proud people of the Kingdom of Benin are born with rhythm in their souls. Music and dance are their lifeblood, a second language through which they express their hopes and fears and joys when words fail.

Above the noises of the night the drums began to throb and hum. The married men led the way, leaping like deer in the firelight. Their wives followed, waving leaves in the evening breeze. Then it was our turn, the boys, all smiles and shining sweat.

Finally, as a yellow-white moon rose above the trees, the girls stepped into the earthen circle. The drums dropped to a wistful throbbing. Like fairies of the forest they danced, a ghostly swirl of blue and bronze. And in their midst, the most beautiful and graceful of them all, danced my younger sister, Banita. I watched until late into the night, transfixed by brotherly love and admiration, as she twisted and swayed to the muffled beat of a drum.

Two

Capture

Banita and I were the only children of Father's second wife, Almonga. Our mother called us her 'moon babies' because we were born exactly a year apart, when the goddess of the moon was swollen with gleaming brilliance. This was a lucky sign, Mother said, and the goddess, Fortune, would guide us for the rest of our lives.

For twelve years the prediction held true. I grew tall and strong and, when I was old enough to understand such matters, I felt the seeds of my father's wisdom growing inside me. Banita was wise, too. But it was her beauty and dignity that made the greatest impression. Although she was only eleven when we celebrated the capture and execution of the Red Man, she was already known in the village as 'Banita the Priceless' – a jewel whose worth was beyond estimation.

But those were our values, reckoned in terms of

goodness and grace. Beyond the hills there were those who thought differently, who had a price for everything, animate and inanimate. Yes, even for Banita the Priceless.

The village remained on the alert for several weeks after the great celebration, worried that more kidnappers would come. But when nothing happened, we gradually fell back into our amiable, easy-going ways. So when the ten-year-old Daudh slept late one morning and failed to climb the lookout-tree as soon as the adults had left for the fields, his brothers and sisters didn't worry too much. They tiptoed past his sleeping form and whispered that no one would mind if he was a little late. There was no hurry: everyone knew kidnappers never came before midday.

But they did. I think they must have been watching the village all night from the edge of the trees. They struck as soon as the singing of the work party had faded away, while Daudh was still asleep and the only creature in the lookout-tree was an old crow that took no interest whatsoever in the drama that unfolded beneath him.

The kidnappers – two men and a woman – seemed to have singled out Banita and myself as a good catch. Silent as snakes, they cleared the wall and crossed the compound to our hut without a soul setting eyes on them. Our doorway darkened and they were upon us, as soundless and swift as the wind. We did not even have time to cry out.

The men, dressed in coarse tunics of brown cloth, were short and ugly. They carried no weapons but relied instead on their speed and immense strength. As I made to stand up and ask who they were and what they wanted, one of them forced a wad of cloth into my mouth. The other seized me by the waist, slung me over his shoulder and made for the door. When I tried to struggle, he squeezed me so tight with his iron arms that I thought I would suffocate.

Across the compound we sped, over the wall and into the shade of the forest – it was over so quickly I hardly realized what was happening. I was angry, terrified and, when I lifted my head to look at the man following us, deeply ashamed. Banita, the sister I was supposed to protect, hung limply over his shoulder like a carcass.

The stamina of our red-skinned captors amazed me. They ran all day with short, powerful strides, pausing only to exchange burdens. As I was the heavier, they took it in turns to carry me – even the woman. She was the same height as the men and just as ugly. Her arms were like gnarled branches and her dark eyes were sunken and dull.

8

If she had ever known pity, it was so long ago that she had forgotten what it was.

The gags in our mouths made speech impossible. All I could do was look into Banita's wide, tear-filled eyes and hope that she understood what I could not say: Be brave, my dear sister! Don't give up hope. We are still together and soon, somehow, we will manage to escape.

At nightfall we reached a small hut on the edge of a clearing in the forest. When we were inside, the kidnappers bound our feet together and removed our gags. They offered us food, but we were too tired and too frightened to eat. This annoyed the woman. She shouted at us in a dialect I only half understood. If we didn't eat, she yelled, we'd become weak and scrawny.

'Then who want you?' she exclaimed scornfully. 'No value. No price. We kill you!'

Her threats made no difference. We left untouched the bowls of broth she brought us. I soon fell into a deep and troubled sleep.

The next day was like the last, except that to begin with we were ungagged. After bumping along on the woman's bony shoulder for an hour or so, we came to a dusty road that ran between thick plantations of palms. Out of the corner of my eye I saw men tapping the trees for their sweet liquor.

This was my chance.

'Help!' I screamed, wriggling desperately to free myself. 'Help! *Kidnappers!*'

With a muttered curse, the women tightened her hold on me and quickened her step. I don't know whether the men heard my cries. If they did, they took no notice. When they were out of sight, we stopped beside a well while the kidnappers stuffed the filthy gags into our mouths again. One of the men then held out a pair of sacks he had been carrying.

'Inside,' he said in a weary, matter-of-fact manner. 'No more trouble.'

I watched in horror as Banita was dropped like a chicken into one of the sacks and the opening was tied with cord. I shook my head violently and tried in vain to wrench myself out of the woman's grip. My arms were forced behind my back, my head thrust forward and I was tipped into a darkness that smelt of sweat and urine.

Three

No Kindly Master

Our kidnappers were like the living dead – soulless monsters under the control of an evil spirit. Their only human feature was their bodies, and even those seemed made of wood or iron. They didn't laugh or cry and they spoke only when they had to. Although we were with them for three days, we never even learned their names.

Late in the afternoon of the third day, we were pulled out of our sacks and made to stand before a tall man dressed in a style of clothes I had never seen before. He wore what I learned later were breeches, leather shoes and a faded blue hat with gold thread round the edges. After staring at us for a few seconds, he nodded and handed some shiny circles of silver metal to our kidnappers. We had been sold. It was the first time in our lives that we had seen money.

As soon as the deal had been done, our kidnappers

disappeared into the trees. Unbound and faced by only a single guard, I wondered for a moment whether I should make a run for it. But after long hours of being bundled in the sack my legs were cramped and aching. I knew I wouldn't get far. Besides, I couldn't leave Banita.

Our new owner seemed to read my mind. 'Wise boy. You and sister now property of Captain Doormie. I not want to lose you,' he said with a smile that displayed magnificent white teeth.

That smile hurt more than all the grunts and rough treatment of our kidnappers. It brought me back into the world of the living, reminding me afresh of our terrible situation. I broke down and fell sobbing into Banita's arms.

Captain Doormie tied a rope round our necks and led us like cattle down a narrow path that led to a village. As we passed between the huts, women looked up casually from preparing the evening meal then returned to their tasks. Even the children playing in the dust scarcely gave us a second glance. They were clearly used to seeing slaves brought in.

In a sort of compound in the centre of the village a band of elderly men came out to inspect us. They were dressed, like Captain Doormie, in strange clothes. One or two carried what looked like long sticks of wood and iron. I know now they were guns that slave traders exchanged for their human wares.

The village elders inspected us like animals at a market, prodding our arms and feeling under our clothes to make sure we were whole and in good health. I had never felt so humiliated in my life. Banita – embarrassed, dishonoured, disgraced – covered her face in her hands and moaned like a creature caught in a trap.

Although it was difficult to understand what the men were saying, they were clearly pleased with us. They laughed and clapped Captain Doormie on the back several times, congratulating him on his 'bargain'. When this little celebration was over, a pair of young men led us away to a large hut on the edge of the compound and pushed us inside.

As our eyes became accustomed to the darkness, we saw that the hut was filled with people. Perhaps three-dozen slaves, men and women, adults and children, were sitting on the floor. They were all bound to each other by the neck.

'Welcome!' said a gruff voice to our left.

'To hell!' added a woman's voice.

At the remark, a low, sorrowful wailing began. I had heard such a sound before. It was the dirge women sang at funerals.

* ★ *

I don't know how long we were held in that crowded hut. It seemed like a year but it was probably no more than a week or two. We were allowed out once a day to wash, go to the toilet and take exercise. Our captors were keen to keep us in good shape – after all, we were the most valuable thing their village possessed. We were so valuable, in fact, that when one man developed a fever he was taken outside and shot. They didn't want to risk the rest of us catching his disease.

Banita and I talked for hours, wondering what was going on back home and promising each other that somehow we would get back there.

'If we are sold to a kindly master,' I said reassuringly on the second day of our imprisonment, 'he may take pity on us and let us go free. I remember Father doing that to a slave once. He said he had to let the man go because he couldn't stand seeing his miserable face any longer.'

Banita laughed. But before she could reply, a man with a gentle voice said, 'Dream, children! But do not have hopes. We do not go to a kindly master.'

I asked him who he was and what he meant. He said his name was Numana and he came from a village near where we were held prisoner. Many of his people had been taken in slavery, he explained, and not one of them had returned. His voice was chillingly sombre.

'Where do they go?' Banita asked.

'Go?' Numana repeated. 'I not know. No one know. But I promise they not come back. Some say they go to the sea.'

'The sea?' I enquired. 'What is the sea?'

Numana took a deep breath. 'Who knows? I no go there before. But they say it like a river with no crossing, wider than all rivers in one river. On and on, for ever.'

'But if it can't be crossed, why do they take us there?' I asked.

'Oh, child!' sighed Numana. 'Your questions I cannot answer. Patience, not me, tells you all you want to know. But I promise the sea is no kindly master.'

That evening, as I lay listening to the villagers chatting over their family meals, I pondered Numana's remarks. Although he had spoken with authority, I could not believe he had been telling the truth. I could not imagine this vast 'sea' that he spoke of; nor could I imagine a world in which there were no kindly masters.

Four

The White Man

We were sold as a group, thirty-three healthy slaves, to a short, fat man with gleaming eyes and a pale brown face that was permanently bathed in sweat. His name was Abdullah, although we soon learned that he preferred another title.

'Abdullah is top trader,' he explained as we stood in the compound, while iron rings were fastened around our necks. 'Abdullah is king of traders. So him you call "Highness". Like a king. Understand?'

No one said a word.

'Abdullah ask if you understand!' he shouted, perspiring heavily.

The boy in front of me turned his head awkwardly towards our new owner. 'Understand, master,' he muttered.

'*Master!*' screamed Abdullah. He stepped forward,

grabbed the chains attached to the boy's iron collar and wrenched him to his knees. 'Bow, slave! Now say what I am!'

'Abdullah is Highness,' the boy mumbled, choking as the rough metal cut into his throat.

Abdullah's fury vanished as quickly as it had arisen. 'Good slave!' he beamed, hauling the boy to his feet again. Abdullah took off the green cloth wrapped around his head and mopped his face with it. 'Slaves, hear two rules of Highness Abdullah,' he went on, replacing his head-dress. 'Rule one – no escape. Escaping slave is dead slave. Understand?'

'Yes, Highness Abdullah,' we replied hesitantly.

'That is good. Rule two – eat plenty food. White Man not want thin slave. Abdullah not want thin slave. Thin slave is dead slave. Understand?'

'Yes, Highness Abdullah,' we chorused once more.

I wanted to ask who this 'White Man' was, but I was afraid. The trickle of blood seeping from under the collar of the boy in front of me confirmed that Abdullah was not the kindly master Banita and I had hoped for. I held my tongue, hoping that the mysterious White Man would take pity on a brother and sister wretched with homesickness.

Abdullah turned out to be less of a tyrant than we had

expected. He had only one interest: getting us to the White Man as quickly and in as good a condition as possible. He fed us well and as long as we remembered to call him 'Highness' and obeyed his rules, it pleased him to treat us like his children. He even permitted us to wrap leaves around our iron collars so they did not chafe our necks. 'White Man want slaves healthy,' he explained with a grin, 'so Abdullah want slaves healthy.'

Day after day we trudged along dusty tracks that took us in the direction of the setting sun. To keep up our spirits, we sang. Each morning men and women from a different tribe took it in turns to lead the singing, repeating the tune and words several times until the whole group knew them well enough to join in. Banita and I were the only people from Benin, and when our turn came we chose the lullaby our mother had sung to us when we were in our cradles. It began:

> *Great Lord Sun, the Magic One,*
> *Protect my children dear,*
> *Great Lord Sun, the Magic One,*
> *Drive out the night of fear.*

After one verse, Banita and I were so choked with tears we could not go on. I noticed that one or two other slaves

18

were also crying. But the tune was an easy one and Numana, who was next in line behind Banita, had already picked it up. 'Great Lord Sun, the Magic One,' he began softly, and soon the whole column, with tears streaming down their faces, was singing Mother's lullaby.

That night Abdullah banned the song. It was, he said, too sad. 'White man want slaves happy,' he declared. 'So Abdullah want slaves happy.'

After a march of many days we came to a wide river. Here we found a great boat of a type I had not seen before: it was not carved out of single tree trunk, like the boats at home, but pieced together out of planks of flat wood. It was driven by long paddles that Abdullah called 'oars'. He explained proudly that he had bought the boat from the White Man. It would take us on the last stage of our journey.

We travelled down the broad, lazy river for about a week. Each day it got wider and wider until one evening I noticed that the left-hand bank had disappeared altogether. The water went on and on, as far as the eye could see.

Alarmed, I reached back and took Banita's hand. 'Where is the land?' I called back to Numana. 'It has sunk into the waters!'

'No, Obah,' he replied ominously. 'I believe it is the sea.

That is the kingdom of the White Man.'

I cannot bring myself to describe in detail what happened next. Even today, when I recall the shock, the pain and the desperate desolation of my soul, I break out in a shivering cold sweat.

Like a trader displaying his wares, Abdullah proudly lined us up on the sandy beach. The first Europeans I had ever seen – dirty men with long hair and unshaven pink-brown faces – assessed us with their cruel eyes. They ordered for us to be unchained and divided into two groups. Our fetters were then refastened and I was rowed through the waves to a gigantic wooden ship that smelled of tar and salt and unspeakable filth. Once on board, we were shouted at and punched and kicked down steep wooden steps into a place more dark and sinister than a tomb.

There, utterly confused and broken-hearted, I sat on the wooden floor, clasped my arms round my knees and howled till my eyes ran dry and my voice was no more than a flutter of dead leaves. I was in hell, and I was alone. On that silver beach bathed in moonlight my little sister, Banita – the jewel whose worth was beyond estimation – had been torn from my arms and carried off screaming into the darkness.

Five

The Crossing

If I ever meet Abdullah again, I'll tell him he was swindled. He sold his slaves too cheaply. The price Mr Spencer, the captain of the *Eagle*, paid for us was so low that he could afford to lose half his cargo on the voyage across the ocean and still make a handsome profit. How do I know this? Because it is precisely what happened.

A slave ship does not belong to this world. It is like a machine sent by the devil, a huge, floating dungeon of evil corrupting everyone that enters it, slaves and sailors alike. The slaves lose all desire to live. All hope, all joy and all faith in humanity is crushed out of them. They are like creatures under torture – their only wish is to be put out of their torment.

Several times on our voyage, during our daily time on deck for exercise and fresh air, a number of slaves tried to leap into the sea to end their misery by drowning. All but three of them were caught before they reached the water. They were beaten with knotted ropes – fifty, one hundred, sometimes two hundred lashes – leaving their backs a bloody pulp of flesh and splintered bone. Not one of them survived their punishment by so much as a week.

Of the three who managed to reach the sea, two, dragged down by their chains, disappeared beneath the waves. The third was recaptured – why Mr Spencer thought it worthwhile sending a boat after him, I'll never understand – and dragged back to the ship for one-hundred-and-fifty lashes. Two days later Numana's crimson, broken corpse was returned to the sea. I mourned my new friend but envied his blessed release from the horrors that still held me captive.

Any excuse served for a beating – sometimes they were given merely to satisfy the cruel whim of an officer. After we had been at sea for about three weeks, a pretty young woman with soft eyes like Banita's vomited when she tried to drink the slime-covered water we were given to drink. The duty officer, a Dutchman named Van Goyen, decided this was an insult. He ordered her to be taken on deck and flogged.

Twenty slaves, myself included, were forced to witness the punishment. I closed my eyes against the torture, but we were forbidden to stop our ears. For ten minutes, with tears streaming down my face, I listened to the woman's anguished pleading, the sobs, the gasps of pain and the regular slash of the rope. After twenty lashes Mr Spencer intervened and ordered the torture to stop. I had mastered only a few words of English by this time, but I got the gist of what he was saying: it was best not to kill such a handsome wench, because some lonely Caribbean planter would pay good money for her.

The conditions on the slave deck were worse than those in which the most hardened criminals are kept. The men and older boys, myself included, were chained together by the legs in rows that ran the entire length of the ship. Until space was created when a number of us died, we did not have enough room to lie down to sleep.

The only toilets were half barrels placed at intervals along the deck. There was no privacy and we were allowed to empty the barrels only when they were full to overflowing. In rough weather the contents slopped over the sides on to the slaves chained next to them. The barrels were too high for the children – yes, Mr Spencer even had young children in his barbarous cargo – and when the ship dipped or swayed in rough weather these poor little things were tipped headlong into the foul waste.

It goes without saying that the stench on the slave deck

was indescribable. Europeans ventured there only with scented handkerchiefs held before their noses. Disease swept through us like dust before a dry wind. It was worst while we lay at anchor off the coast of Africa, waiting for the last of the consignment of slaves to arrive. Perhaps fifty men, women and children died while we sweltered in the tropical heat. After one dreadful night, fifteen bodies were slung over the side into the cool green ocean. Captain Spencer didn't seem much alarmed – that afternoon, forty-six fresh souls came aboard to take their places.

I mentioned earlier that a slave ship corrupts slaves and sailors alike. Now that I have seen much of the world, I know that wickedness and goodness are spread evenly throughout all peoples and nations. But evil is like an infection – unless it is checked, it spreads, especially among the weak and poor, from one person to another.

So it was with our crew. Looking into their eyes, I saw that deep down few of them were truly evil men. But they were afraid: afraid of their officers, afraid of their fellows and afraid of Captain Spencer. And he, I believe, was afraid of himself. And in this atmosphere of fear, evil flourished.

Although most of his victims died shortly after their punishment, Captain Spencer ordered only one man to be flogged to death. He was not a slave, either, but a member of Mr Spencer's crew, a cabin-boy named Jack. His crime? Giving part of a fish he had caught to the mother of a dying slave girl.

After Jack's flayed body had been tossed over the side, Mr Spencer addressed his assembled crew. By then I had picked up enough English on the ship to understand most of what Mr Spencer said. His speech went something like this: 'There is no place for a soft heart on this ship. Sentiment lines the road to mutiny and ruin. Our cargo is a blessing, something that God in his infinite wisdom and mercy has given the white man for his pleasure and enrichment. Give thanks to the Almighty, therefore, and let's have no more foolish sentiment.'

Six

Fresh Food

People often describe a terrible situation as a nightmare: something too awful to be real. That is not how I felt on board the *Eagle*. My pain and hopelessness were horribly genuine. It was my previous life that felt unreal. My world had been turned inside out – it was as if my childhood had been a dream and I had now woken to find that reality was not smiles, laughter and a thousand small kindnesses, but starvation, disease and beatings.

I was crushed by despair. Hardly a moment passed on that dreadful ship, that floating hell, when I did not wish myself dead. The sense of hopelessness, like the stench of the dark hold where we were chained, increased with each passing day. I wanted each sleep to be my last; I hoped each rotten meal and every foul drink would poison me; I prayed that each sunrise would herald my final tortured day on earth. Death was no longer a feared

26

enemy – it was a friend I longed to visit.

But the friend never came.

After almost two months at sea the *Eagle* sailed into a broad and beautiful harbour surrounded by green hills beneath which nestled a small town. When the sails had been stowed and the anchor lowered on its rusty, rattling chains into the blue waters of the bay, we were ordered on deck, forty or so at a time. Still chained, we were made to strip naked and tip canvas buckets of sea water over each other. It was only the second or third opportunity we had had to wash since leaving Africa. Captain Spencer wanted to offer clean goods for sale.

As the cool, salty water ran down my body, I felt a change come over me. I was being given a fresh start – my mind as well as my body was being cleansed. I had survived, I told myself, because I was meant to survive. From that moment onwards, I decided to work *with* the forces that controlled my life, not *against* them. I resolved to put my depression behind me and seize every opportunity, no matter how slender, to free myself and seek out Banita. I was sure that, like me, she had been taken to this New World and was still alive. My only duty was to find her, rescue her and take her home.

While we were washing, I was surprised to see a number

of small boats set out from the shore and make for the *Eagle*. I was even more surprised when these boats were tied up alongside and about a dozen men clambered up the ladders hanging over the ship's sides and came aboard.

They were a strange-looking group, not at all like the scrawny sailors I had become used to. Mostly large and middle-aged, they wore bushy beards and broad hats beneath which their eyes glinted like dark shells. These fleshy-faced men, I realized later, were overseers seeking fresh labour for their sugar and tobacco plantations. They had come aboard at the earliest opportunity to preview the goods that would be appearing in the slave market the next day.

The planters poked, pinched and prodded us as if they were inspecting dead meat. Eventually, still chatting and joking as if they were the only human beings present, they clambered awkwardly into their boats and were rowed back to the shore.

As we were being herded back down to the hold for the night, a shiver of panic ran through the people ahead of me. It grew to a sullen muttering, then quickly rose to a howling and shrieking. The men shouted angrily, stamped their bare feet on the planking and rattled their chains.

Suddenly, a group of about eight men, fastened together by their ankles, made a dash for the side of the ship.

Someone on the deck above fired a shot. The leader of the band fell to the deck, moaning and clutching his stomach. Undeterred, his friends tried to drag him with them towards the sea. The sailors moved in quickly, laying about them with clubs and whips. They beat the men mercilessly into line and drove them, still dragging the body of their wounded comrade, down the stairs and into the darkness below.

On joining them, I learned what the disturbance had been about. Ullan, who had picked up more English than most of us, had asked a sailor who the visitors from the shore were. He was told that the bearded strangers were cannibals. The next day, the sailor said, Captain Spencer would sell us to them as fresh food.

I now realize that the sailor was only making a grim joke. But at the time, how were we to know this? We knew only our African ways. Bitter experience had taught us that Europeans were capable of any cruelty, any barbarity. They had never explained why we had been shipped across the rolling ocean. We believed we were to be sold as slaves, but could not be certain. Remembering how the planters had pinched and prodded us, therefore, it was easy to believe they had been examining something to eat.

Later that evening the howling and rattling started up

29

again. We made such a din, and the timbers of the ship shook so violently that I feared they would fall apart. The noise must have alarmed Captain Spencer, too, for he sent the first mate below to find out what the trouble was.

'Don't worry, slaves,' he laughed when he learned the cause of our protest, 'no one's going to eat you! You've come 'ere to work. Work till you drop. And when you do, they'll stick you in the ground and we'll bring over some more. Now shut up!'

Although the words were hardly encouraging, they calmed our worst fears. That night, lulled by the lapping of the waves against the side of the ship, I renewed the vow I had made earlier: somehow, anyhow, I had to escape.

Seven

The Beat of a Drum

We were woken at dawn the following morning and taken ashore in a variety of small boats. Six African slaves rowed the one I was in. One of them, a huge fellow with muscles like boulders, looked kindly at me.

Leaning forward into his stroke, he smiled and said in an African tongue I could only just understand, 'Boy, welcome Barbados!'

My heart jumped. I hadn't seen anyone smile like that, openly and frankly, for weeks. It was a beam of sunlight into my dark world.

'Thank you,' I replied in my own language.

The man nodded.

'Barbados, is it a good country?' I asked eagerly. 'Are you happy here?'

The man's eyes darkened. 'Happy? Slaves happy?' Seeing my look of disappointment, he added, 'If gods smile on you, OK. But if you find bad master, it better you die on ship.'

Our conversation was cut short by a shout from a white man who stood at the stern with a musket across his chest: 'Hey, Jacob! I said no talking to the new slaves!'

The friendly oarsman raised his head and called out in a voice that was half-jovial, half-sarcastic, 'Yes, Mr Edwards!' Then, looking back towards me, he said quietly, 'No more talk, boy. But Jacob hope the gods smile on you.'

I was surprised to hear the oarsman called by such a strange name. Later, I learned that slave-owners refused to use African names. They renamed their slaves – 'christened', they called it – with names of their own choosing. It was a way of showing that we were their property. This was not a custom we followed in Africa, where names were considered sacred.

Once ashore, we were roped together and led through the streets of the town. I stared about me in amazement at the tall houses with painted doors and glazed windows, the like of which I had never seen before. I saw horses for the first time, too, and carriages and water pumps and other mysteries. On a street corner I saw my first European ladies: an elegant pair in long gowns who shaded themselves from the sun with bright parasols. They were so still and stately that I thought they were some kind of doll.

The sight of the women and houses and machines set me thinking again about how confusing these white people were. How could they be so clever and yet so cruel? Were they gods or devils? At the time I couldn't make up my mind. But later, after I had thought about it, I decided they were neither. They were different from us in only one respect: greed. Greed, an unquenchable thirst for wealth, had driven them to invent and discover; it had also driven them to regard fellow human beings as mere objects to be bought, sold and beaten. In their hungry eyes we were, like their machines, simply a means of getting wealth.

Near the centre of the town, which I learned was called Bridge Town, we were locked in a large room – men, women and children all crowded together. When we had been there about an hour, guards brought us food and water. They were less rough than the sailors and the meal they provided – fruit and some kind of sweet bread – was better than anything we had tasted on board ship.

After eating we lay down on the earth floor. It was very hot and before long I closed my eyes and fell asleep. As often happened, I dreamed of my village. I smelt the scent of the blossom in the trees, tasted the rich food, saw the

33

graceful figure of Banita dancing in the firelight to the beat of a drum . . .

The beat of a drum? I sat up, not knowing whether I was asleep or awake. Although the visions had faded, the sound of the drum remained, throbbing through the thick tropical air like a heartbeat. What sort of cruelty was this, I wondered, that tortured me with the sounds of the life I had lost?

The doors of the room opened and the guards entered. 'Get up!' they shouted. 'You heard the signal! That drum means the slave market will be open in fifteen minutes. The first batch is needed in the yard straight away.'

Without caring how they divided us – friend from friend, parent from child, husband from wife – they singled out about twenty men and led them away. The rest of us stood about anxiously, wondering what was going on.

Half an hour later the guards returned and led off a second batch of slaves, myself included. We were shepherded into the corner of a dusty yard in the middle of which was a wooden platform. Around it, smoking pipes and chatting, stood some two-dozen planters. I recognized several of them as the men who had come aboard the *Eagle* the previous day.

An auctioneer climbed on to an upturned crate and called for silence. Four male slaves were led on to the platform and the bidding began. As the prices were called out and the slaves taken away by their new owners, I looked around the planters. One, a plump fellow with a red face and blue eyes, looked as if he might be a kindly master. I hoped he would buy me rather than the lean, stone-faced man who stood next to him.

When my turn came, the blue-eyed man opened the bidding. I smiled and looked at him encouragingly. This seemed to annoy stone-face, who put in a higher bid of his own. Blue-eyes responded with a still higher price. Stone-face looked grim and raised the bidding once more. At this the blue-eyed man shrugged and shook his neighbour's hand to congratulate him on his purchase. I had been sold for twenty pounds.

'Who is my master, sir?' I asked the overseer who led me by the arm to a group of slaves gathered on the far side of the yard.

'Your master?' he replied with a laugh. 'Why, it's Mr Gramolt. I hear he's a bit of a tyrant. It's too late now, boy, but you'd have been better off staying in Africa!'

Eight

Iron-heart

I was one of six slaves that Mr Gramolt bought that day. Apart from myself, four were grown men and the other a young woman, Olliana, whom he wanted as a house slave. As soon as the auction was over, our new master came over to us and stared at us for a full five minutes from beneath the brim of his black hat.

Eventually, speaking in a high, sharp voice, he said slowly and deliberately, 'I have bought you. You are mine and I am your master. You are here to work, nothing else.' With that, he gave some instructions to the two slave-drivers he had brought with him and left the yard.

While he was speaking, one of the slave-drivers had lit a fire in a brazier and thrust an iron rod into the flames. At first I thought the fire was for cooking and we were going to be given a meal before setting out for Mr Gramolt's plantation. I was painfully disillusioned.

The drivers tied our hands behind our backs and made us kneel before the brazier. Only when one of them pulled the iron, now red hot, from the fire did we realize what was happening. We were going to be branded.

When the slave at the end of the line saw the driver lift the flaming iron, ready to burn its shape into his flesh, he let out a roar of horror and struggled to get to his feet. Immediately, the second driver, who was standing behind him, lashed out with a long leather whip. The thongs cut across the man's back and neck, leaving vivid red weals on his bronze skin.

The man fell to his knees again and looked round in pained surprise. As he did so, the first driver thrust the glowing iron on to his shoulder. The man screamed with pain. The smell of smouldering flesh rose to my nostrils and I felt sick with disgust and fear.

With more whipping and crying, the brander moved along the line of kneeling slaves, fixing each with the unmistakable 'G' of Gramolt. When my turn came, to lessen the pain I tried to concentrate on happier times. I closed my eyes and thought of my mother and Banita standing hand in hand outside our home...

The moment the branding iron touched my left shoulder, the image disappeared in a swirl of searing pain. The fire seemed to be burning right through me. I cried out and raised my right hand to push it away. But by then the brander had already moved on to the person next to me and my fingers felt only the disfiguring welt of smouldering skin.

I carry the scar to this day. I think of it now, however, not as standing for 'Gramolt' but for 'God' – the Great Father who sees all and understands all, and who will, one day, punish most terribly those who have offended against His laws.

Gramolt's plantation was more than twenty miles from Bridge Town. Roped together and watched over by the drivers on horseback, we walked some of the way that evening, slept in the open and finished the journey the following morning. We had no shoes and our feet, softened by the weeks on board ship, were cut and bleeding by the time we reached our destination.

Our master was a rich man. His estates, completely given over to sugar cane, stretched as far as the eye could see along a broad green valley between rolling hills. He lived in a white-painted mansion, larger than any dwelling I had ever seen, set on a slope that overlooked his entire property. A narrow brown road ran from the tall gates of his gardens to a group of smaller, single-storey houses further down the hill. This was where the slave-drivers and their families lived.

Lower still, beside a small stream, stood a line of ramshackle wooden huts with thatched roofs – the slaves' accommodation. This was where we were taken on our arrival at the plantation. Shortly afterwards, an elderly African woman appeared and, without a word, led Olliana up the road towards the master's house.

One of the drivers, named Barclay, left the men in a hut in the middle of the line and led me to a smaller one on the end. 'This is your new home, boy,' he explained. 'There are eight of you, the weeders.'

In broken English I asked what the word 'weeders' meant.

'You'll find out tomorrow, boy,' Barclay retorted, sounding annoyed at my ignorance. He leant down from the saddle and pointed to a board nailed beside the door. It had some sort of writing painted on it.

'You'd better learn your new name,' he said. Running his whip down what was obviously a list of names, he read them off with difficulty. 'Moses – no, he's still with us. Josh-u-a, Adam, Isaac, er, Sol-o-mon, Sam-u-el . . . Was that the one that died? Yes. *Samuel.*'

He swung round and poked me in the chest with his whip. 'You – are – Samuel,' he said slowly. 'Got it?'

I nodded. 'Right. You'll find some food over there.' He indicated a small hut beside the stream. 'The others will be back at nightfall. I'll see you in the fields at dawn. And, Samuel, God help you if you're late.'

By the time I fell asleep that night I had begun to wonder whether it wouldn't have been better to have died on the *Eagle*. My fellow 'weeders' – the boys responsible for weeding between the sugar canes – were pleasant enough, especially Joshua. But they told me I had been brought to the harshest plantation on the whole of Barbados.

Gramolt, known throughout the island as 'Iron-heart', was indeed a tyrant. The only good thing about his plantation was the food, which was considered better than elsewhere. Otherwise, the place was terrible. The slaves worked from dawn to dusk six days a week – seven if they were behind with their tasks. The discipline was ferocious: the weeders received two strokes of the whip for missing a single weed, six for laziness and goodness knows how many for cheek or rebelliousness.

With a sinking heart, I asked whether anyone had managed to escape.

Adam, a thin lad with an ugly-looking rash on his face, grabbed me by the arm and explained in halting English, 'Listen, Sam: even if you get away from plantation, you not get off this island. Nobody escapes. Only one place you go when you leave here, Sam, and that's to the grave.'

Nine

The Preacher

The next morning we were woken at first light, given a hasty breakfast of bread and bananas, and divided into three work parties. A driver then led the party I was in down a twisting track to the fields and immediately set us to work. Having taken almost no exercise for several weeks, by midday I was exhausted. My back ached, my hands were sore and blistered, and my neck burned from exposure to the blazing sun. By the evening I was so tired I hardly had the energy to stagger home. I fell asleep the moment we reached our hut and didn't wake until the following morning.

As the days passed and I became fitter and stronger, I came to see life on the Gramolt plantation as a kind of war: myself against the slave-drivers. Their aim was to make me a slave in mind as well as body. They didn't just want me to work. They wanted me to be like one of their horses, a

42

dumb creature that couldn't think for itself. This was my battle. I worked as a slave because I had no choice; but I was determined never to think as a slave. The drivers, I resolved, would not put out the tiny lamp of hope that burned in my heart. I would rather die than let that light be extinguished.

The fight was long and hard. As I had been warned, Gramolt's drivers were harsh task-masters. In the first week, inexperienced in the work of weeding, I received a dozen strokes of the whip for failing to do my job properly. Barclay called this process 'breaking me in'. The beatings left my back so raw and painful that for a month I had to sleep lying on my front.

In time, though, the punishments became less frequent. Sometimes I escaped the whip for weeks on end. This was not just because I knew what was expected of me. Gramolt (whom we saw only when he made his weekly inspection of the plantation) had paid good money for us and he reduced a driver's wages if he beat a slave so severely that he could not work. This ensured that there were no floggings as murderous as those on board the *Eagle*. Only if a slave tried to escape, we were told, would he be beaten to death. Since no one had ever tried, we did not know whether this was just a threat.

The most powerful weapon I had to fight against was

not the whip but the spirit-sapping drudgery of our labour: up at first light, breakfast, a long walk to the fields, toiling in the sun for five hours without a break, lunch, back to work until evening, the weary trudge back to our huts, supper and sleep. So it went on, hardly ever varying, day after day, week after week, month after month.

Sunday was generally a rest day. We slept, played games and tended the little gardens in which we grew extra fruit and vegetables. Towards evening we gathered beside the stream for music, singing and dancing. These were the happiest and yet also the saddest of times. Most of the slaves on Gramolt's plantation had been born in Africa and so carried within them the rhythms of their homeland. For six days of the week these were bottled up inside them. But on Sundays they burst forth like blossoming flowers into a brilliant medley of sound and movement.

It was the custom for each new slave to teach the others a song from his African home. When my turn came, I didn't know what to choose. As several of the slaves were from Benin, though not from my region, all our favourite songs were already known. Eventually, after much teasing and cajoling, I decided to try the lullaby that Banita and I had sung while prisoners of Abdullah.

As I stepped into the circle of eager faces gathered

around the fire, a drum began to beat. I clasped my hands together and began to sing. '*Great Lord Sun, the – Magic – One, Protect . . .*' My voice cracked and died. Blurred images of my family danced in the flames of the fire. Sobbing uncontrollably, I bowed my head and shuffled off into the darkness.

Although many others spoke kindly to me afterwards, Joshua was the first to console me.

'Don't worry, Sam,' he said kindly, putting a hand on my shoulder. 'It happens to almost everyone the first time.'

'Only the first time?' I sniffed. 'Oh, Joshua, I don't ever want to sing that song with dry eyes. I don't ever want to forget!'

'I understand,' my friend replied, 'but sometimes it is best to forget. It takes away the pain.'

I lifted my head and looked at him. 'Maybe, Joshua,' I said. 'But when I feel no pain, I will be dead.'

One Sunday morning, almost a year after my arrival in Barbados, a strange European appeared before the slave huts. A tall, bony man, he wore a white tunic that fell like a dress down to his shiny black boots. After climbing on to a tree stump, he took a deep breath and cried out, 'Brothers and sisters, I come with good news!'

Amazed that a white man should call us his 'brothers and

45

sisters', and inquisitive about his good news, we gathered round to hear what he had to say.

The man was a preacher. For the next hour he spoke to us of Jesus Christ, God the Father, everlasting life in heaven, the importance of loving our neighbours, and other aspects of his Christian faith. He finished by teaching us a hymn, which we all joined in heartily. When this was over, he asked in a loud voice, 'Brothers and sisters, do you want to be Christians?'

The Christian world that the preacher spoke of seemed so far removed from our wretched world that a number of slaves cried eagerly, 'Yes! Yes! We do, sir!'

The preacher wrote down their names in a little notebook and promised to return the next Sunday to teach them how to pray. 'That way,' he explained, 'your souls will be saved and you will go to heaven!'

Later, we talked a good deal about what we had heard. Several of the boys had liked the preacher and looked forward to his return. 'I will try to love the drivers now,' exclaimed Adam, 'so I can go to heaven with Lord Jesus!'

I was not so sure. One remark in particular had confused me. When asked whether Mr Gramolt was a Christian, the preacher had replied eagerly, 'Of course! Your master is a very good Christian gentleman.'

That didn't make sense to me. Buying, branding and

46

beating struck me as a very peculiar way of showing love for one's neighbours.

Ten

Escape

The preacher changed my life for ever, although not in the way he or anyone else expected. Little Adam, as thin and scabby as ever, became the preacher's keenest disciple. He took to crying, 'Praise the Lord!' and, 'Hallelujah!' at least fifty times a day and tried to persuade others to join him in special prayer meetings. His fellow slaves were tolerant, but not so the drivers. Adam's zeal irritated them and they frequently whipped him for speaking out of turn or spending too long at his lunch-time prayers.

Matters came to a head one hot and sultry Monday afternoon. Adam and I were working alongside each other, clearing the weeds between rows of young cane shoots. As usual, Adam was singing a hymn.

'Stop that noise!' Barclay suddenly shouted from the end of the row. 'It's getting on my nerves.'

Adam did as he was told and we worked on in silence.

Five minutes later, however, he began singing again.

'*Sssh!*' I hissed. 'Be quiet, Adam! You'll get into trouble!'

Adam stopped hoeing and looked at me. 'I was singing a hymn, Sam?' he asked.

'Of course you were! Now get back to work before Mr Barclay sees you.'

Adam resumed his hoeing for a short time, then stopped again. 'Samuel,' he said, sounding strangely excited, 'if I was singing without knowing it, then I was inspired. The word of God was speaking through me. Praise the Lord – I am a prophet!'

To my amazement, he stood up and cried, 'Mr Barclay, sir! I am a prophet! Hear ye the word of the Lord!'

Before I could stop him, he began running towards the startled driver, trampling the young cane underfoot and waving his hoe wildly above his head.

I don't know whether the slave-driver really thought he was being attacked, or whether he just wanted an excuse to teach the poor boy a lesson. The whip snaked out, caught Adam round the neck and threw him to the ground. With the lad at his mercy, the bully lashed at him most cruelly, covering his frail body with a lattice of gaping cuts. Each blow was accompanied by a horrible curse.

Adam did not resist or cry out. Instead, speaking in a

49

feeble, choking whisper, he repeated between the lashes, 'God bless you, Mr Barclay. God bless you, sir!'

It was more than I could stand. A force beyond my control took charge of me. Without thinking what I was doing, I raised my hoe and brought it down with all my strength on the driver's head. There was a loud crack, his knees crumpled and he fell to the ground beside his astonished victim.

Too horrified to move, I stared at the driver's motionless body. Adam's thin voice brought me to my senses. 'Oh, Samuel,' he whispered, 'what have you done? Run away! Please, *run away!*'

I glanced about me. We were some distance from the rest of the gang and no one had yet noticed what had happened. Seized with panic and not thinking where I was going, I dropped my hoe and fled towards the trees on the edge of the field.

I ran blindly, through the trees, across a track, along the bank of a stream and up the wooded slopes that overlooked our plantation. On and on I went, pursued by images of slavering dogs and men armed with gigantic whips. At last, near the crest of a hill, I could go no further and collapsed on to some soft earth beneath a canopy of leaves.

I listened for the noise of my pursuers – the baying of dogs and the shouts of the men. Instead, I heard only the cries of birds and the light pattering of an afternoon shower on the trees overhead. I had not been followed.

Unsure what to do, I decided to make for Bridge Town. After all, I told myself, it was through this port that I had come on to the island, so it ought to be possible to leave it by the same route. The lamp of hope, all but extinguished a few minutes previously, now burned more brightly.

For three days, living off the land and keeping away from all habitation, I followed the road to the coast. On a hill above Bridge Town I rested and planned my next move. News of my escape had certainly reached the port ahead of me and, dressed in torn rags, I was bound to attract immediate attention. I decided, therefore, to enter the town at night and find a hiding-place near the harbour.

Looking back, I realize it was a hopeless idea. I hadn't gone more than a few hundred yards, creeping along in the shadows, before I was spotted by a watchman on the opposite side of the road. He ordered me to stop and identify myself.

I panicked and darted into a narrow lane. Behind me, the watchman began ringing his alarm bell and calling for assistance. Immediately, a group of three or four sailors appeared at the far end of the lane. I turned. The watchman, now accompanied by several others, was advancing towards me. There was no escape.

My captors carried lanterns and stout sticks. They advanced steadily towards me, spreading out in a circle as they did so. Expecting a rain of blows, I fell to my knees and covered my head with my hands. Rough fingers grabbed my shirt and tore it away at the shoulder to reveal the branded 'G'.

'Thought so,' said a voice. 'It's the one from Gramolt's what attacked his driver. Come on, let's get him under lock and key.'

I lowered my hands, lifted my head to face the watchman and said as calmly as I could, 'Mr Gramolt will beat me to death, sir.'

'That's none of my business,' replied the watchman. 'Get up!'

As I rose to my feet, I explained, 'Yes, I hit my driver. But I was protecting a poor boy, half-crazy. He said he was prophet and—'

'Oh, shut up!' interrupted the watchman. 'Save your story for old Iron-heart.'

Eleven

Captain Collins

I had often thought how wrong Mother had been when she predicted that Banita and I would be guided by the goddess, Fortune. For two years Fortune had totally abandoned me. But now, just when I needed her most, she mysteriously reappeared in the form of a neat-looking gentleman in a blue coat.

'One moment, please, watchman!' said the stranger, stepping forward and looking at me very earnestly. 'I would like a word with this boy.'

The watchman raised his lantern and, recognizing the speaker at once, nodded his agreement.

'Tell me, boy, what were you saying about a prophet?' asked the blue-coated gentleman.

Heartened by the man's sincere manner and honest voice, I told him what had happened between Adam, Barclay and myself. When I had finished, he turned to the watchman and asked, 'This scoundrel of a slave-driver didn't die, did he?'

'No, Captain Collins,' replied the watchman, 'though I heard he needed many stitches in his head.'

'Good,' answered the captain. 'Then my mind is made up. I will buy this slave, here and now.'

The onlookers let out a gasp of astonishment. 'But he's not mine to sell, Captain,' complained the watchman. 'He belongs to Mr Gramolt.'

The captain smiled. 'I know that. And I know Mr Gramolt's love of money, too.' Turning to me, he asked, 'How much did he pay for you, boy?'

'I think it was twenty pounds, sir,' I replied, unable to believe what was happening.

The captain took out his purse. 'Then I'll pay Mr Gramolt double. It'll save him the trouble of having to flog the wretch to death.'

As he was speaking, Captain Collins counted out forty pounds into the watchman's hand. He gave him an extra coin to cover his expenses and told him to take the money directly to Mr Gramolt and explain what had happened. If the plantation owner didn't accept the bargain, he concluded, he would know where to find him.

'And where might that be, Captain?' asked the

bewildered watchman, slipping the coins into an inside pocket.

Leading me by the arm, the captain was already walking swiftly down the lane towards the harbour. 'On the sea, watchman!' he called over his shoulder. 'On God's glorious ocean!'

After taking me back to his ship, the captain gave orders that I was to be washed, fed, given a new suit of clothes and left to sleep for as long as I wished.

When I finally awoke, I became aware of a familiar rolling motion. Startled, I found my way on deck and stared about me. Bridge Town and Barbados were nowhere to be seen. Having left port at first light, we were out of sight of land and hissing through the blue-green ocean beneath a brilliant tropical sun.

'Boy, come here!' called someone from the deck above where I stood. Looking up, I saw Captain Collins at the ship's wheel. I scrambled quickly up the stairs and fell on my knees before him.

'Thank you, sir!' I cried, feeling tears welling up into my eyes. 'Thank you and bless you, sir!'

'Get up, boy!' said the captain crossly. 'Don't ever kneel before another man – only God is to be worshipped!'

★ ★ ★

My saviour, as I secretly called Captain Charles Collins, was one of the most honest and virtuous men I have ever met. He and his crew on the schooner *Dolphin* showed me a different type of white man. Before this, I had believed all Europeans to be either cruel, like the slavers and planters, or simply blind to our suffering, like the preacher. But these people were different. They believed that everyone, black and white, slave and free, was God's creature and deserving of respect. Not surprisingly, there were no floggings on board the *Dolphin*.

My new companions hated injustice. Most of them believed slavery was wrong and wanted to see it abolished. This view stemmed from their strong religious faith.

The captain and several of his crew belonged to a group of Christians known as Quakers. They didn't swear or drink alcohol, and they had little respect for anyone in a position of power. Keeping themselves to themselves, they devoted their simple, hard-working lives to the glory of God. The only thing I didn't like about them was their belief that music and dancing were sinful. Consequently, no matter how grateful I was to the captain for rescuing me, I was never tempted to become a Quaker myself.

When I learned of the captain's faith, I realized why he had rescued me. It was not just because he felt sorry for me, but because I had stood up for Adam when he had believed himself a prophet. 'God moves in mysterious ways, Samuel,' the captain had explained one day. 'Who are we to say that poor Adam was not indeed a mouthpiece of Our Lord?'

During our first conversation on the bridge of the *Dolphin*, Captain Collins made a bargain with me. (The Quakers' religion, I soon learned, did not prevent them from being very astute businessmen.) He had paid a lot of money for me and, although he wouldn't treat me as a slave, he would not yet agree to part with me. However, as he did not like the idea of owning another person, he would let me earn what money I could by trading as we went from port to port around the Caribbean. When I had saved the forty pounds I had cost him, I could pay it back to him and become a free man.

I accepted the arrangement immediately. It was better than anything I could have hoped for. As a free man, with papers signed by the captain to prove it, I would be able to go where I wanted. And I knew full well where that was: I would trace the ship that had carried Banita to the New World, find where she was working, buy her freedom and return home with her to Benin.

Twelve

The *Dolphin*

I soon thought of the *Dolphin* as my home, the first I had known for almost two years. Sometimes I compared it with my first home in Africa. Although both were close-knit and friendly, the *Dolphin* came off worse in two respects: it was a community largely without either music or females.

Captain Collins permitted singing only rarely, usually at the end of a long voyage. As for women, the only one we ever saw on board was Mrs Collins, who occasionally accompanied her husband on a short journey. She took little pleasure from such trips. Indeed, I sometimes wondered if she knew what pleasure was. Her thin, pale face and grey eyes gave the impression that life was for enduring, not enjoying. As I, too, had felt that way only a short time ago, I pitied her.

I was known on board as 'Sam the Cabin-boy' to

distinguish me from 'Sam the Cook', another ex-slave. Soon after I had joined Captain Collins' crew, I asked him whether I might be called by my original name, Obah.

After thinking for a moment, the captain replied, 'No, I think you should remain "Samuel". We have become used to the name. Besides, the original Samuel was a prophet.'

Although I was disappointed by this reply, I was far too grateful to the captain to argue with him.

My work as cabin-boy was not difficult. As the personal servant of the captain and his three officers, I had to clean and tidy their cabins every day and run errands as they wished. For this I was paid one guinea at the end of each month.

When we were at sea I had generally finished my regular work by midday. To begin with I spent the afternoons chatting with the crew or fishing with a line over the side of the ship. I soon became bored with this routine, however, and looked around for something else to do.

The answer was provided by Christopher Hardy. A young man of about twenty, Christopher was Captain Collins' nephew. He had been forced to abandon his university studies because of some mysterious 'indiscretion' (Sam the Cook said it involved the young wife of a very senior politician) and had been taken in hand by his uncle for 'reformation' and a chance to make his fortune.

Christopher had taken an immediate liking to me. I believed he sensed that, like him, I did not have much of the Quaker in my soul. One afternoon, finding him sitting on deck reading a book in the shade of the main mast, I asked him what he was reading.

He glanced about him and said quietly, 'Don't tell my uncle, but it's a novel.'

'What's a novel?' I asked, not having heard the word before.

'It's a story of adventure and romance. Not very improving of the mind, but dashed good fun!'

I liked the sound of a novel. 'Do you think, Mr Christopher, that I could ever learn to read it?' I asked.

The young man flicked back a wave of fair hair from his brow and exclaimed brightly, '*Ever*, Sam? Of course! An intelligent fellow like you could learn to read it in no time. Blow me! Why didn't I think of this before?' He jumped to his feet and set off for the stairs that led below deck. 'Come along, Sam! Lessons are starting right now, and I don't want you late for school!'

So it was, guided by the flamboyant Christopher Hardy, that I learned to read and write the English language. What my young teacher lacked in skill, he made up for with enthusiasm. As he had predicted, I was a quick learner and within six months was able to read the Bible (at Captain Collins' insistence) and write a fair letter.

The ability to read and write had an enormous impact on me. It opened my mind to new ideas and led it down paths I had not known existed. More than I realized at the time, it began to alter the way I thought about myself and the world.

The change was brought home to me most sharply one Sunday evening. The *Dolphin* lay at anchor off Kingstown, Jamaica. I was seated at a table I had brought on deck, practising my writing by the light of a candle. As I scratched and scribbled with my pen, I became aware of a familiar sound drifting across the still waters of the harbour. It was the steady beat of an African drum.

I stood up, went to the side of the ship and stared at the point from where the sound was coming. On the beach I made out a large bonfire. Around it, moving gracefully to the rhythm of the drummer, figures were dancing. The slaves who worked in the port, men and women who had so little to be joyful about, were celebrating their day of rest.

As I watched, a woman began to sing. The sound touched my heart. It carried me back to Gramolt's plantation and further back still, to a village far, far away.

Disturbed, I glanced down at the pen I still held in my hands, then back at the table, inkstand and paper on which I had been writing my name, Samuel. The singer's voice had confused me. Was I really Samuel the Cabin-boy? Or was I Obah, the boy from Benin? I did not know.

I walked back to the table, sat down and wrote *Samuel* and *Obah* next to each other. With the music still in my ears, I stared at the two names for a long time. Which one was I? Eventually, unable to decide, I took up my pen and wrote beneath them a third name.

Yes, that was the answer. It didn't matter what I was called. Whoever I was, Samuel or Obah, I still had a duty to fulfil. I glanced again at the last name. A picture of a young girl rose before my eyes. She was pleading, begging me to help her. *Banita*.

Thirteen

Freedom

I had accepted Captain Collins' scheme to buy my freedom without thinking about it carefully. Money was almost unknown to me and I had never bought or sold anything in my life. Nevertheless, after I had been on the *Dolphin* for eight weeks and had saved two guineas, I tried my hand at trading.

At our next port of call, a small town in the Bahama Islands, I went into the market and bought five hundred fish-hooks. They had, I was told, just arrived from Britain and were of the finest quality. They cost me a whole golden guinea.

A week later we were in Havana on the Spanish island of Cuba. I went ashore with my hooks and, having found a likely-looking stall near the harbour, I showed my merchandise to its half-Indian owner. Since he spoke very little English, we had great difficulty understanding each other. Eventually, though, after much haggling, we reached an agreement. I exchanged my hooks for six silver Spanish coins' worth, the stall-owner assured me, 'one-guinea-an-haff'.

Delighted at my success, I hurried back to the ship and told Christopher how I had got on.

'Sounds good enough,' he smiled. 'Let's see the coins.'

I showed him the six pieces of silver. He eyed them suspiciously, lifted one to his mouth, bit it and said grimly, 'Oh, dear, Sammy! You've been swindled. If those coins were genuine they'd be worth about half a guinea, which would be bad enough. Trouble is, they're false. They're forgeries, made of silver mixed with some other metal.'

Devastated, I retired to my hammock and vowed never to trade again. In my misery I even considered running away. I could have slipped off the *Dolphin* in any of the ports we visited and was sure Captain Collins would not have come looking for me. Nevertheless, I rejected the idea almost as soon as it came into my head. It hurt me even to think of betraying those who had rescued and befriended me. Besides, I would still have been a runaway slave, branded and without money or papers.

It was Captain Collins, not Christopher, who persuaded me to change my mind about trading. When he gave me my third guinea and asked whether I had started trading yet, I told him of my disaster in Havana.

He shook his head and said kindly, 'Ah, well! There are a good many rogues in this world, Samuel, as you know only too well. But do not give up. Listen, I have a plan that might help you . . .'

Many slave-owners permitted their slaves to earn a little money by selling things they made in their spare time, such as beads and carvings. The workmanship was sometimes of a very high standard. Captain Collins suggested that I could buy the slaves' handiwork for a fair price and sell it for a small profit to merchants going to Europe. He believed some of the pieces, particularly carvings of animals, would fetch a good price in the Old World.

The scheme worked better than I had expected. I started cautiously, buying six lions carved by a slave who was too old to work in the fields and selling them to a friend of Captain Collins who was returning to England. I made a shilling out of the deal. From this simple start my little business grew steadily until, by the end of the year, I was close to saving the forty pounds I needed to pay for my freedom.

My business brought me much more than money. I made new friends among the slave community who, when I told them of my plan to track down Banita, provided me with invaluable information. Abdullah sold his slaves to only two men, Captain Spencer of the *Eagle* and Captain Tennant of the *Charity*. As my sister had not been with me on the *Eagle*, she must have crossed the Atlantic in the *Charity*.

On Montserrat I finally met a woman who had been on the *Charity* with Banita. My sister had survived the voyage, the woman told me, and had been sold as a house slave to a Mr Tunstall from the colony of Southern Carolina in America. This news was doubly exciting. Not only was Banita alive but, as a house slave, there was a fair chance of her being treated well.

During the *Dolphin*'s next visit to Charleston, South Carolina, I enquired after Mr Tunstall. No one had heard of him, or, if they had, they were not prepared to tell me. I did not stay ashore for long because the whites in Charleston were very hostile to black people and I was afraid of being kidnapped. I returned to the *Dolphin* angry and frustrated. Nevertheless, I now knew where to resume my search.

Captain Collins looked surprised when I entered his cabin one morning and presented him with a small leather bag containing forty pounds.

'So soon, Samuel,' he said, sounding slightly

disappointed. 'You have done well, haven't you? You are not only the best cabin-boy I've ever had, but you have the makings of a merchant, too. I hope, when you are a free man, you will not think of leaving us.' He paused, then added quietly, 'You see, Samuel, you have become almost a son to me.'

I had not been expecting this. 'I am deeply honoured, sir,' I stammered. 'I would love to stay . . . But I have a sister, sir, who needs me . . .'

The captain raised a hand. 'Yes, I have heard of your wish to find your sister. It's a very Christian mission, Samuel, and one I respect. Tell me, though, what will you do when you find her?'

'I'll set her free, sir!' I exclaimed.

'Indeed, Samuel! How?'

Slightly embarrassed, I blurted out, 'Anyhow, sir! I will do whatever it takes.'

The captain smiled and pushed my bag of coins across his table towards me. 'I think, Samuel, that this will be of greater use to you than to me. Come, take it back.'

Fourteen

The Last Stage

I do not know the exact day of my birth because in Benin we did not consider such things important. We lived as natural creatures do, guided by the seasons, sun and stars, and kept no record of dates or days of the month. Nevertheless, when I moved into the European world and heard them talk of birthdays, I began to wonder when mine was. With Christopher's help, I guessed that it must have been in April. I chose the 15th because that was the day on which I was formally released from slavery.

Captain Collins called the crew on deck, made a short speech and handed a sheet of parchment to me. It declared to the world that as from 15 April 1768 Samuel Collins, once of Benin, Africa, aged sixteen, was a free man. Not having a surname of my own, I had willingly adopted the captain's as a mark of my respect and gratitude to him. After a few prayers, we all went back to work.

That night, Christopher invited me to his cabin and we celebrated my freedom in a less religious manner – with tots of rum from a bottle he kept hidden under his bunk.

I agreed to remain with the *Dolphin* until her next visit to Charleston. To my frustration, we remained in the Caribbean for another three months before finally sailing into Charleston harbour one steaming hot afternoon in mid-July. The next morning, I said goodbye to Captain Collins, Christopher and the crew of the *Dolphin*, thanked them a thousand times for all their many kindnesses, and went ashore.

Before going into the town, I stood on the quay and watched the *Dolphin* raise her anchor, hoist her sails and slip noiselessly away to sea. I did not realize until that moment quite how attached I had become to that well-ordered, righteous ship. It had been my home, my security. Now, although free, I was completely and utterly alone.

A young, well-dressed African confidently striding down the main street towards the governor's offices was an unknown sight in Charleston, a shabby, prejudiced town. White men and women stopped and pointed at me. One or two hissed. I took no notice – I was a free man and a subject of King George along with the best of them. I could do what I wanted. Or so I thought.

At the governor's offices I hoped to find someone who could tell me where Mr Tunstall lived. When I reached my destination, I found a large notice beside the door that read: *NO NEGROES PERMITTED*. I hesitated for a moment, then walked up the path and rang the bell.

The door was opened by a pasty-faced young man whose yellow skin was dotted with angry pustules. 'Go and tell your master to come himself,' he barked. 'When you learn to read, you'll understand the sign says "No Negroes permitted".'

'I have no master and I can read,' I said angrily.

'God strike me blind! An educated savage!' replied the young man with exaggerated surprise. 'We don't want your sort around here. Get off with you before I call the army!'

As he made to shut the door, I stuck out my foot to prevent it closing. At this, the young man began shouting for help, saying he was being attacked by a mad Negro. The din went on for almost five minutes before the door was pulled back to reveal two red-coated soldiers standing before a portly gentleman wearing a wig that was several sizes too big for him.

'Name?' said the gentleman in the wig, keeping well behind the soldiers.

'Samuel Collins,' I replied.

'Proof?' went on the inquisitor.

'Proof of what?' I asked.

'Proof of your name, dunderhead!'

I took out the parchment Captain Collins had given me and passed it between the soldiers to the official. He read it quickly, then shook his head. 'Invalid unless stamped,' he sniffed.

'Then, as this is the governor's office, would you be good enough to stamp it for me?' I asked, trying hard to remain patient.

'Costs five guineas.'

'*Five guineas!*' I retorted. 'What man can pay—'

'Goodbye!' interrupted the official. He turned to go.

'No, wait!' I called. 'Here are your five guineas.'

I took the money from my purse and handed it to him. No sooner had I done so than the soldiers slammed the door in my face. Furious, I hammered on the door until the head of the portly official appeared at an upstairs window.

'If you don't go away this instant, slave,' he said coldly, 'I will order the soldiers to shoot you dead. That is not a threat.'

I knew from the tone of his voice that he meant it. Burning with shame and anger, I walked slowly back towards the harbour. In the eyes of the swindling official, and no doubt of every other white person in the town, I was still a slave. And there was nothing I could do now to prove otherwise.

On my last visit to Charleston I had bought some driftwood carvings from Louis, an old boatman who lived with the other harbour slaves in a rough cabin near the shore. Not knowing where else to go, I made my way towards the cabin.

Louis was delighted to see me again. He had news for me, too. Three weeks previously, a man by the name of Tunstall had passed through the port on his way home from a trip abroad.

'What is more, Sam,' the old man grinned, 'Mr Tunstall's slaves told old Louis where their master's farm is. It's a hundred miles from here, near a place they call Eutaw Springs.'

I was so grateful to Louis that I didn't have the heart to tell him I wouldn't be buying his goods any more. Instead, I paid him two shillings, four times the asking price, for a carved elephant. Then, directed towards the house of a man who wouldn't mind selling a horse to a Negro and then teaching him how to ride it, I set out on the last stage of my journey.

Fifteen

Banita

On leaving old Louis, I was followed through the streets by a crowd of boys who hooted and threw stones at me. Outside a church a constable stopped me and asked why I was causing such a disturbance. I escaped arrest only by paying him two guineas and promising to leave town immediately.

The man Louis said might provide me with a horse and riding lessons was a toothless Frenchman named Gaston. He ran a sort of run-down inn on the track that led to the interior of the colony. I spent my first night there and in the morning asked him about a horse. Saying he might be able to help me, he led the way to a field in which grazed half a dozen of the leanest, mangiest creatures I had ever seen.

Two hours later, poorer by five pounds, ten shillings, I was in the saddle and riding slowly up the dusty track that led to Eutaw Springs. Gaston had promised me I would have no difficulty managing my horse, Pouvantail, because she was one of the gentlest creatures ever born. This was an exaggeration. Only by kicking till my legs ached could I get her to move at all, and even then she never managed more than a slow walk.

I took eight days to reach Eutaw Springs. It was not a pleasant journey, and each day my dislike of that bleak, barren land grew. I was afraid of its snake-infested swamps and slow, oozing rivers. I shivered in its dark forests that were cold even at the height of summer. I was bored by the sameness of its empty spaces, the meanness of its little hills and its shallow, apologetic valleys.

Not surprisingly, few people lived there. Those that did took on the ungenerous, dull character of the countryside around them. To be honest, after my experiences in Charleston I had expected little difference. I was convinced, as I still am, that South Carolina and all its inhabitants were cursed.

Even so, I had one cause for joy as I rode through that wretched land. The further I moved inland, the more familiar the name of Mr Tunstall became.

'Yes,' replied a pair of sour-faced woodcutters from whom I asked directions on the fourth day of my journey, 'there is a Tunstall at Eutaw Springs. A farmer of some sort. Got money, too.'

Two days later, stopping at a cabin beside a place where the road divided, I found a young woman digging vegetables in her garden. Mr Tunstall's was that way, she declared, pointing to the left fork without lifting her head from her work.

'Thank you, ma'am,' I replied. 'You don't happen to know, ma'am, whether Mr Tunstall is married?'

'He is,' said the women, still not looking at me.

'And Mrs Tunstall has slave girls to help her in the house?'

'Two, I think.'

'And have you seen them?'

'Aye, but some time ago.'

Perplexed by the woman's timid, offhand manner, I said, 'Excuse me, ma'am, but would you mind looking at me?'

The woman stopped her digging and raised her head a little. 'My husband says I'm not to look at black men,' she explained nervously. 'Please go on your way.'

'I will ma'am,' I said, wondering what sort of monster she was married to. 'But first, please tell me whether one of Mrs Tunstall's slave girls looks a little like me.'

The woman shot an anxious glance in my direction. 'Yes, a little. There, you know now. Please be gone. My husband may be back at any moment.'

Thanking the woman warmly, I dug my heels into Pouvantail's sides and set off again towards Eutaw Springs. My heart was pounding. I wanted to shout and sing with delight. Banita, my sister! After all this time, I had found her!

It seemed impossible, yet it was true.

The track that led to Tunstall's farm branched off the road to the right before it reached Eutaw Springs. The turning was marked by a tidy wooden board with the word *TUNSTALL* painted on it in large white letters. I had already decided on my plan of action. I would ride straight up to the farm house and, if possible, speak to Mrs Tunstall myself. I still had plenty of money to offer for Banita's freedom. If it was not enough, I would go away and earn more. I would collect whatever sum she wanted, as long as she would let my sister go.

Riding over the brow of a low hill about half a mile from the road, I came across the charred remains of a large wooden house. Only the stone chimney was still standing. The rest of what had clearly been a substantial mansion was just a twisted and tumbled mass of blackened timbers. As ashes were still blowing in the wind, I guessed the fire to have been quite recent.

Nearby, staring at the ruin, stood an elderly black man dressed in the rough clothes of a slave. I dismounted and went over to talk to him.

'Excuse me, sir, but whose house was this?' I asked.

'Master Tunstall's,' came the reply.

My heart jumped. 'No one hurt, I hope?'

The man lifted his face to mine and I saw that his eyes were red with weeping. 'The master and mistress escaped through the window,' he said. 'But not the slaves. It was night, you see, and they was locked in. My wife was one of them. All burned.'

I could manage only one word. 'Banita?'

'Missy Banita? The pretty one? She's over there, sir. Lying all peaceful at the last.' He pointed to a row of six newly dug graves in the garden of the house.

The world went dark. Although the man continued speaking, his words meant nothing to me. I heard only a loose board flapping in the wind against the chimney. A regular, rhythmic, almost musical sound. Like the slow, sad beat of a drum.

Historical Notes

There had been no slavery in Britain itself since the twelfth century and there had always been men and women who thought slavery in the colonies to be unjust and immoral. Their first target was the slave trade. By the 1780s a powerful anti-slave trade movement had emerged, backed by religious groups such as the Quakers. Its most prominent leader was the evangelical MP, William Wilberforce.

In 1807, after much debate, the British parliament finally banned the slave trade. Between 1781 and 1807 the trade had reached a grizzly climax, with British ships carrying over a million slaves from Africa to the Americas. In 1833 parliament passed the Emancipation Act, which outlawed slavery itself in all British colonies.

Meanwhile, other nations had abandoned the slave trade, the USA in 1809, France in 1814 and Spain and

Portugal in 1820. Slavery itself was less easily done away with. It lingered on in France's colonies until 1848 and in the USA until 1863. It was completely outlawed in Brazil only in 1888.

The abolition of slavery and the slave trade in no way solved the many problems they had created. This was perhaps most noticeable in the USA, where in many southern states men and women of African descent, African Americans, continued to be treated as second-class citizens until the 1960s and beyond.

Further Information

If you would like to know more about the slave trade, these are among the many books on the subject:

Courtauld, Sarah, *The Story of Slavery* (Usborne, 2007)
Equiano, Olaudah, *The Interesting Narrative and Other Writings* (Penguin, 2003)
Grant, R. G., *Slavery* (Dorling Kindersley, 2011)
Lyndon, Dan, *Black History: Africa and the Slave Trade* (Franklin Watts, 2013)
Steele, Philip, *Documenting History: Slavery and Civil Rights* (Wayland, 2011)

There are also many websites about slavery. A few are listed below:

www.spartacus-educational.com/slavery.htm
www.bl.uk/learning/histcitizen/campaignforabolition/ abolitionbackground/abolitionintro

Glossary

Auctioneer Someone who manages an auction, selling goods to the highest bidder.

Benin An ancient, West-African kingdom.

Brand To make a mark on flesh by burning.

Cannibal Someone who eats human flesh.

Colony Overseas territory owned and governed by another country.

Compound An enclosed space between several houses.

Constable A law officer, an early policeman.

Dirge A slow, sad song, often sung at funerals.

Emancipation Act The law that abolished slavery in all British colonies (1833).

Evangelical A Protestant Christian who believes that human beings can be saved only by faith revealed in the Bible.

Guinea An old English coin worth one pound and one shilling.

Inkstand A freestanding container for ink.

Old World Europe.

Overseer A superintendent or steward – someone who keeps an eye on the work of others.

Parasol A sunshade in the shape of an umbrella.

Parchment A strong kind of paper used for formal documents.

Plantation A large farm on which crops like sugar, cotton and tobacco were grown.

Planter The manager of a plantation.

Prophesy A prediction of what will happen in the future.

Prophet Someone who foresees the future or, in the Bible, has a special relationship with God.

Quakers A popular name for the Society of Friends, a Christian group that believes each individual communicates directly with God without the need of a priest.

Schooner A swift, two-masted sailing vessel.

Shilling An old English coin worth one twentieth of a pound.

Slave-driver A man responsible for overseeing a gang of slaves at work.

Tyrant A ruler or master whose power is not limited by law, so they can do what they want without interference or objection.

Other titles in the Survivors series:

AFRICAN SLAVERY
A YOUNG BOY'S STORY

9780750296359

WORLD WAR I
A YOUNG BOY'S STORY

9780750296366

THE HOLOCAUST
A YOUNG BOY'S STORY

9780750296427

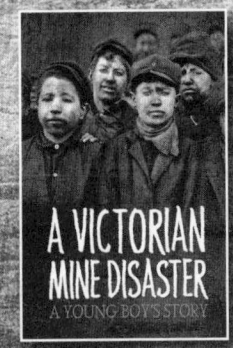

A VICTORIAN MINE DISASTER
A YOUNG BOY'S STORY

9780750296434

WORLD WAR II
A YOUNG GIRL'S STORY

9780750296298

THE GREAT DEPRESSION
A YOUNG GIRL'S STORY

9780750296304